First published in 2010
by Wayland

Text copyright © Karen Wallace
Illustration copyright © Jackie Harland

Wayland
338 Euston Road
London NW1 3BH

Wayland Australia
Level 17/207 Kent Street
Sydney, NSW 2000

Series Editor: Louise John
Editor: Katie Powell
Cover design: Paul Cherrill
Design: D.R.ink
Consultant: Shirley Bickler

A CIP catalogue record for this book is available from the British Library.

ISBN 9780750263375

Printed in China

Wayland is a division of Hachette Children's Books,
an Hachette UK Company

www.hachette.co.uk

The sun was coming up over the farmyard. Suddenly there was a loud noise.

"Honk! Honk! Honk! Someone has stolen my egg!" cried Goose crossly.

Detective Dog pricked up his ears. There was another mystery to solve!

He ran across the farmyard
and looked down at the
empty nest.

"Keep your feathers on,
Goose," said Detective Dog.
"I'll find your egg."

First Detective Dog looked
all around the farmyard,
but he did not see the egg.

Then he went to see Cat.

"Have you seen Goose's egg?"
Dog asked Cat.

"No," said Cat. "But Magpie
did tell her that she had made
her nest in a very silly place!"

"What do you mean?" asked
Detective Dog.

"Don't ask me," cried Cat.
"I'm not a bird. I don't
make nests."

Detective Dog thought hard.
What did Magpie mean?

So he went back to Goose's nest to have another look.

Detective Dog soon spotted the problem. Magpie was right. Goose HAD built her nest in a silly place, at the top of a steep hill.

The egg must have rolled out
of the nest and all the way
down the hill!

Detective Dog put a round
stone into Goose's nest.

It began to roll down the hill.

THUD! The stone bumped into
Duck as she sat on her nest.

"Quack! Quack!" cried Duck, jumping up into the air.

A big white goose egg was sitting in her nest.

"You thief!" honked Goose.
"You stole my egg!"

"I did not steal your egg,"
quacked Duck. "I found it by
my nest so I looked after it."

"Woof! Woof! Quiet, please!"
said Dog. "Duck did not steal
your egg, Goose. You made
your nest in a silly place.
The egg rolled out and went
down the hill."

Suddenly, there was a loud
CRACK!

The big white egg broke open
and a fluffy gosling came out.

"My baby!" honked Goose.
She folded the gosling into
her wings.

"I'm so sorry I called you
a thief, Duck," cried Goose.
"Thank you for looking
after my egg."

"And thank you, Dog,"
honked Goose. "You're
the cleverest detective
in the world."

"Cheep!" agreed the gosling.

START READING is a series of highly enjoyable books for beginner readers. **The books have been carefully graded to match the Book Bands widely used in schools.** This enables readers to be sure they choose books that match their own reading ability.

Look out for the Band colour on the book in our Start Reading logo.

The Bands are:

Pink Band 1A & 1B

Red Band 2

Yellow Band 3

Blue Band 4

Green Band 5

Orange Band 6

Turquoise Band 7

Purple Band 8

Gold Band 9

START READING books can be read independently or shared with an adult. They promote the enjoyment of reading through satisfying stories supported by fun illustrations.

Karen Wallace was brought up in a log cabin in Canada. She has written lots of different books for children and even won a few awards. Karen likes writing funny books because she can laugh at her own jokes! She has two sons and two cats.

Jackie Harland is woken up every morning by her two cats taking it in turns to nibble her toes and pat her face with their paws. It works every time, and they always get their breakfast first. In spite of that, she loves them very much, and after she finally gets to eat her own breakfast, she loves painting, especially animals.